Yugen

Yugen

Mark Reibstein

ART BY

Ed Young

books for young readers

NEW YORK • OAKLAND • LONDON

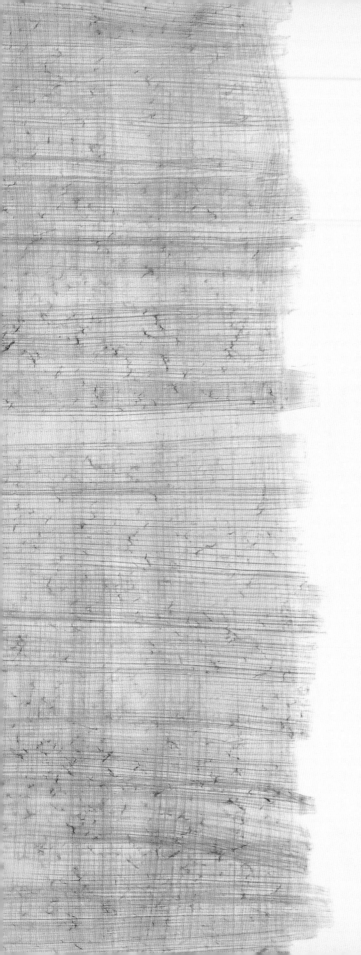

A TRIANGLE SQUARE BOOKS FOR YOUNG READERS FIRST EDITION

SEVEN STORIES PRESS

140 Watts Street

New York, NY 10013

LIBRARY OF CONGRESS CATALOGING-IN-PUBLICATION DATA

Names: Reibstein, Mark, author. | Young, Ed, illustrator.

Title: Yugen / Mark Reibstein ; illustrated by Ed Young.

Description: First edition. | New York : Seven Stories Press, [2018] |
  Series: Triangle square books for young readers | Summary: Illustrations,
  simple text, and haiku reveal a young boy's longing and remembrance of his
  mother.

Identifiers: LCCN 2018023638 | ISBN 9781609808655 (hardback) | ISBN
  9781609808662 (ebook)

Subjects: | CYAC: Loss (Psychology)--Fiction. | Mothers and sons--Fiction. |
  Cats--Fiction. | Haiku. | BISAC: JUVENILE FICTION / Social Issues /
  Emotions & Feelings. | JUVENILE FICTION / Family / Parents. | JUVENILE
  FICTION / Stories in Verse.

Classification: LCC PZ7.R262 Yug 2018 | DDC [E]--dc23

LC record available at https://lccn.loc.gov/2018023638

Printed in China.

1 3 5 7 9 8 6 4 2

Dedications

To:
A return to Meanings,
lost while searching
for Truth.
—ED YOUNG

For Nenette, because with you I love my life . . .
—MARK REIBSTEIN

Come,
sit by me
in the snow
here,
under this
black sky,
the moon
so gold.

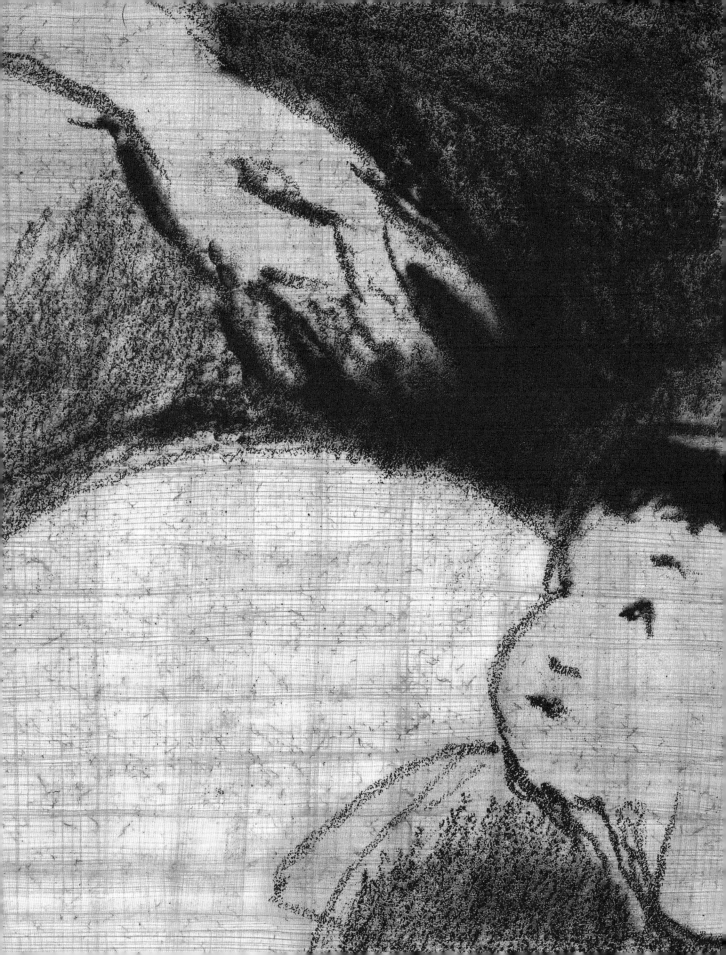

I'm Eugene—
"Yugen" to my mom,
who held me tight
when the wind
blew cold.

That cat there—
spotted white and gray,
sniffing
the night air—
is Hatsuay.

We once had Shinji
(they were named
for lovers),
but he's since
run away.

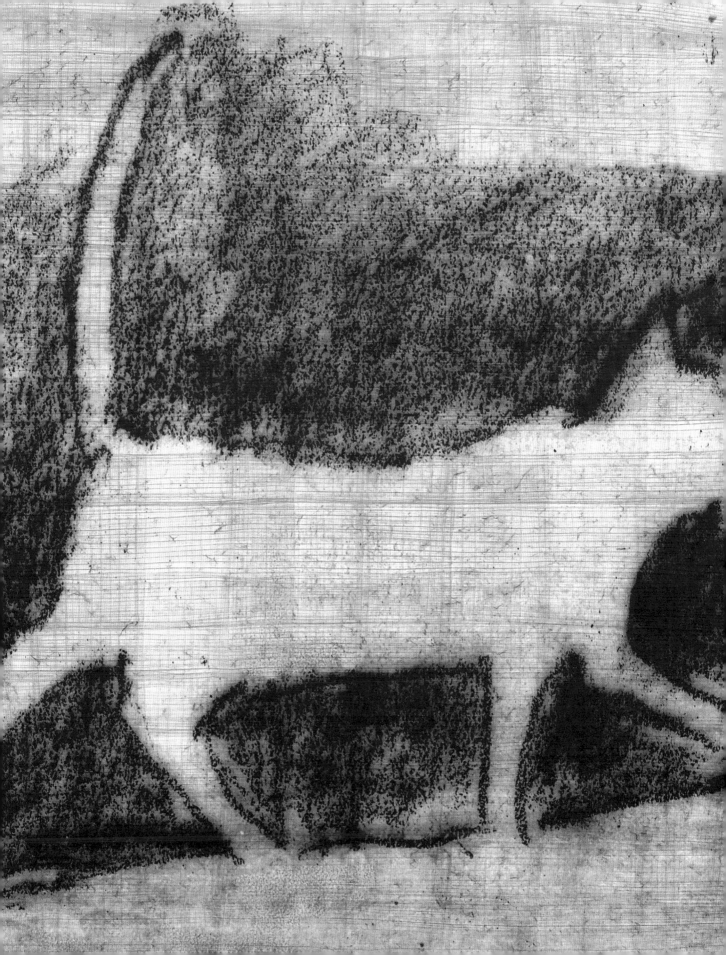

Those dark trees there
whisper memories;
that cherry's my
mom's favorite.

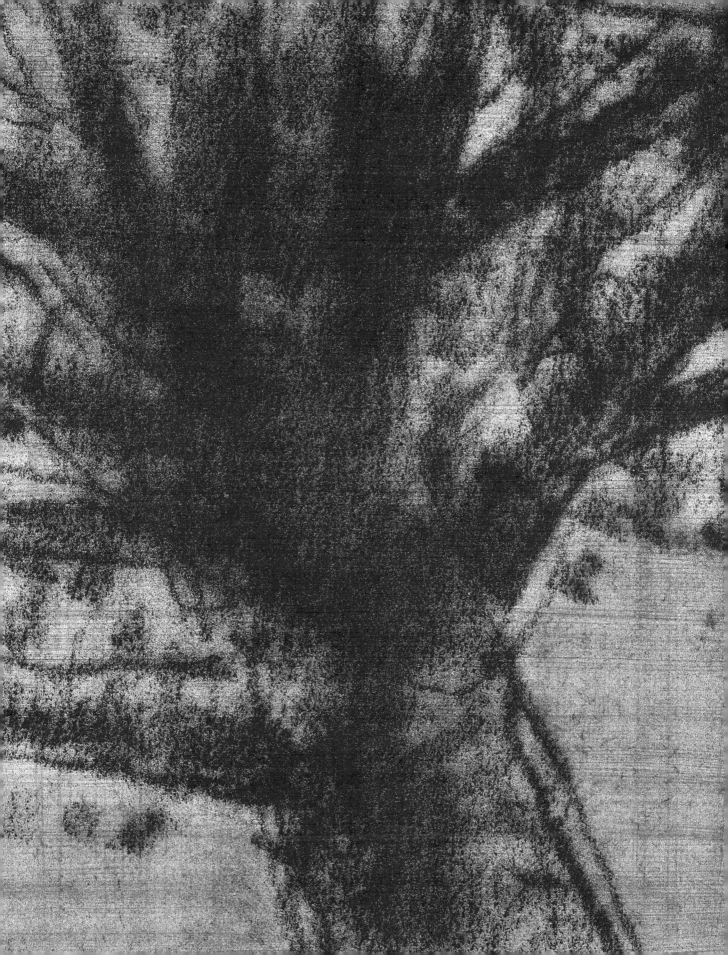

When its
April-petals
fell like snow,
we watched
from blankets
under it.

Mom said
everyone stops work
to watch
cherry petals fall,
in Japan.
Born there,
she went back once,
but since
I couldn't go
too, we made
a plan.

At the same time,
both of us
would look at
the same solitary star.
Sitting in the blue night,
seeing it together,
we'd be close,
though far.

On nights like this
she'd say,
"Let's go to Japan!"
and pour a deep hot bath.
We'd both climb in
and then she'd sing,
washing my back
with a warm,
wet cloth.

Now she's gone again—
I think Shinji
went to find her;
he left
in June.

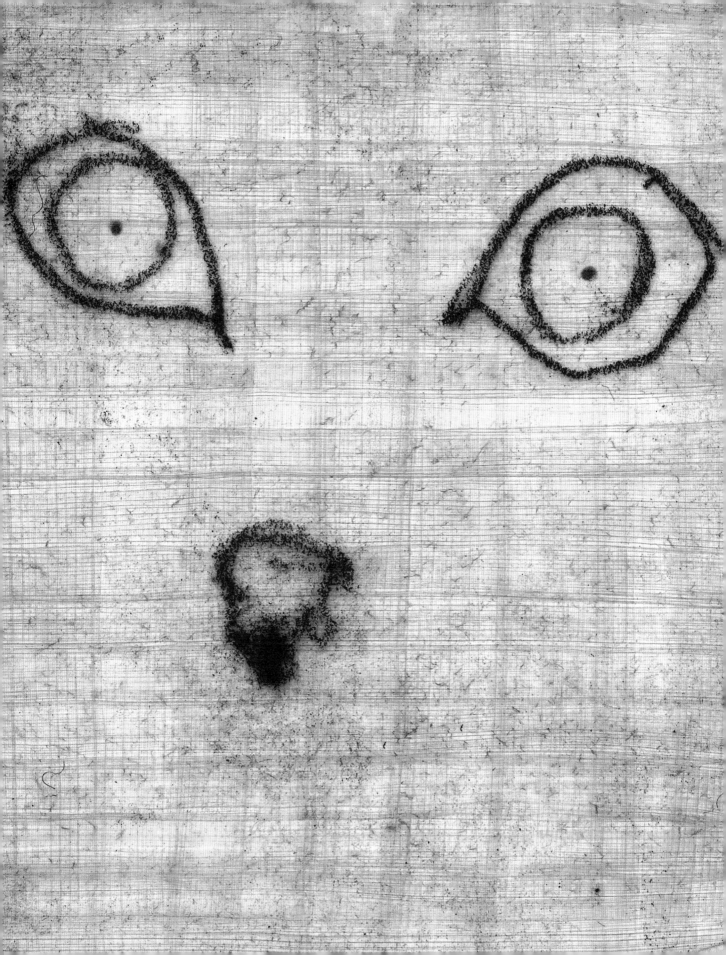

Since then,
Hatsuay and I
come out each night
to wish upon
the moon.

We say,
"Please shine
a path
for lovers
and mothers,
to guide them
back home."

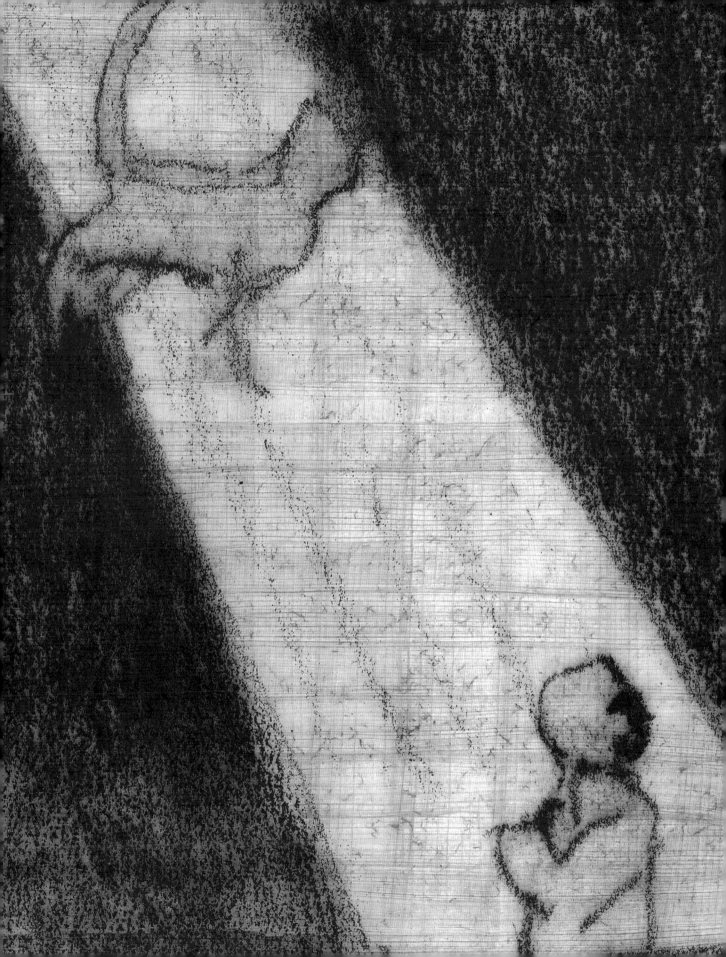

Inside,
I bathe and
Hatsuay
purrs,
as if there's a secret
she knows.

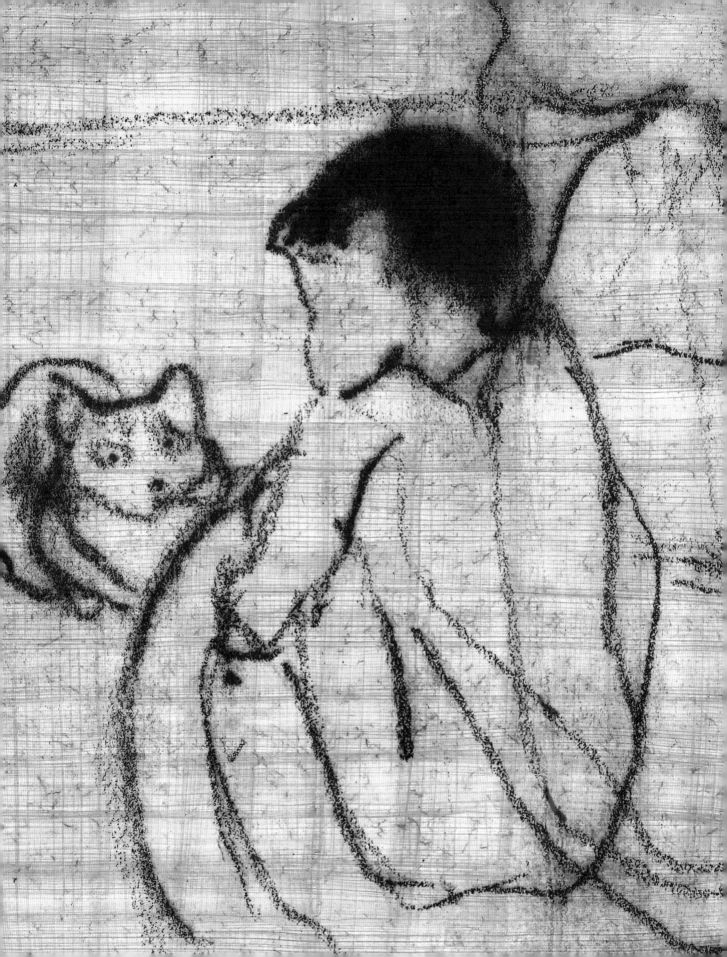

She's learned it
from watching
starlight fall
and flower on the
silver snow.

Author's notes

"Yugen" is a Japanese term for the "subtle and profound."
It comes from the word for "dim" or "deep" and it suggests
that a few brushstrokes can awaken many thoughts and
feelings. Zeami, the originator of Noh theater, used natural
imagery such as the "subtle shadows of bamboo on bamboo"
or "snow in a silver bowl" when describing it. He called it
a "profound, mysterious sense of the beauty of the universe"
and the "sad beauty" of human experience.

The text of *Yugen* consists of seventeen American
Sentences. The American Sentence is a seventeen-syllable
form, based on the haiku, invented by the American poet
Allen Ginsberg.